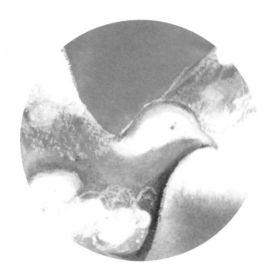

On Wings of Light

On Wings of Light

Meditations for Awakening to the Source

co-created by JOAN BORYSENKO, PH.D.,
and JOAN DRESCHER

WARNER BOOKS

A Time Warner Company

Warner Books, Inc., 1271 Avenue of the Americas, New York, NY 10020

 A Time Warner Company

Printed in the United States of America
First printing: October 1992
10 9 8 7 6 5 4 3

LIBRARY OF CONGRESS CATALOGING-IN-PUBLICATION DATA

Borysenko, Joan.
    On wings of light : meditations for awakening to the source / co
-created by Joan Borysenko and Joan Drescher.
        p.   cm.
    ISBN 0-446-39255-3
    1. New Age movement. 2. Meditations. I. Drescher, Joan E.
II. Title.
BP605.N48B67   1992
291.4'3—dc20   92-13761
                                                                        CIP

Book design by Giorgetta Bell McRee
Cover design by Julia Kushnirsky
Cover illustration by Joan Drescher
Back cover photo by Jean Abbott

DEDICATION

To Celia Thaxter Hubbard
aka "Mother Goose"
whose friendship and love
of art, beauty and the Sacred Mystery
encouraged me to
spread my wings and fly.

—*Joan Borysenko*

To my mother, Elizabeth McIntosh Lizer
who read to me as a child,
the stories of magic and beauty
and helped my creative spirit to fly

and to

Harlan Lizer
for his love and inspiration.

—*Joan Drescher*

ACKNOWLEDGMENTS

From Joan Borysenko

Special thanks to my husband, Myrin, who supported this project with love, enthusiasm and an eagle eye, and to our children Natalia, Justin and Andrei.

Thanks to the circle of women whose love helped awaken my memories: Celia Thaxter Hubbard, Robin Casarjian, Peggy Taylor, Elena Burton, Rachel Naomi Remen, Tricia Lovett Stallman, Elizabeth Lawrence, Carolina Clarke, Lauren MacIntosh, Yvonne Drew, Leslie Kussman, Olivia Hoblitzelle, Jane Alter, Renée Summers, Phoebe Lonberg and Vickie Poppe.

The sweetest of thanks to my co-creator Joan Drescher who helped make this project such a delight.

Thanks to those whose wisdom and love inspired the text: Stephen Maurer whose respect, kindness and caring helped me to heal and led me to believe in and know my Higher Self, Stephen Levine from whose books I learned the lovingkindness meditations that have so enriched my life and this book and to Jon Kabat-Zinn whose teachings of mindfulness have informed my work and whose friendship has been an awakening; and a special tribute to my eleventh-century mentor and guide The Abbess Hildegard von Bingen: Scientist, Physician, Mystic, Artist and Awakener of the People.

From Joan Drescher

A special thanks to my husband Ken for always being there with love and support, and to our children Lisa, Kim and Ken.

To my kindred spirit and loving friend Joan Borysenko whose words became one with my art.

Thanks to Myrin Borysenko for his vision, friendship and encouragement with all projects.

The circle of women that Joan B. mentioned above and to Anita Olds, Joanne Cavatorta, Margot Cheel and Syma—all midwives of vision and beauty.

Ron Moir whose guiding spirit is always present and to all his family, especially Tia and David.

And from the bottom of both our hearts thanks to our agents Helen Rees and Myrin Borysenko, our editor Joann Davis and to Warner Books for their willingness to support the production of a new genre of book. We also thank Warren Dillon for providing a warm and wonderful art studio for Joan Drescher, and Pam and Hal Dohrman for the loan of their "shackteau" in Paradise which inspired some important changes in the text. Thanks also to the many people we have not named whose lives and work encouraged us to create a book that heals.

INTRODUCTION

This is a book about remembering what we have always known in our hearts
but forgotten in our minds.

That
Behind all appearances
Beyond the illusion of separateness
we are One
With ourselves, with each other and
With the supernal Light of Creation.

Bridges between Spirit and matter

We are the agents, the channels, the beings
Through which Love manifests in this world.
In this remembering lies our destiny
our hope, our joy and our healing.

In those moments when we lose ourselves in the colors of the sunset, the eyes of a child, or the sweetness of the morning bird song, our hearts open and our spirits soar. Our bodies feel relaxed and alive. Our senses quiver. We feel connected to a larger whole. In these moments our creative juices flow and we feel both powerful and loving. We have come to some deeper part of our being, a part which is in touch with a greater wisdom than our personal store of knowledge, a part that is universal.

This part of us has been called by many names: the Self, the Higher Self, the intuition, the Essence, the Divine Spark. It is characterized by serenity, compassion, wisdom, gratitude and love. Most of the time the Self lays hidden behind a layer of clouds like the sun. Those clouds are made of the fear that we are not lovable — by ourselves, other people or the Divine itself. Too often we create life stories that revolve around guilt, shame and blame and sometimes it seems as though the sun in our hearts will never shine again. We have forgotten who we really are. This is a book for remembering and bringing new stories of love and healing into our own lives and into this fragile, magnificent planet that we all share.

Joan Drescher and I loved working on this book together because the entire process was a remembering for us. It was fun, joyful, delightful and full of serendipities and surprises. Both of us were quite familiar with the process of writing. Joan Drescher has written and illustrated more than twenty-five children's books. I have published two books, Minding the Body, Mending the Mind and Guilt Is the Teacher, Love Is the Lesson. The usual process of creativity for both of us has been a "mixed bag" somewhere between the extremes of Divine inspiration and having a root canal done. This book, in contrast, was a pleasure throughout, and more than that, an awakening for us both.

The seeds of our collaboration were planted in a "former life" when I was an Instructor in Medicine at Harvard Medical School and Director of a Mind/Body Clinic at one of the Harvard teaching hospitals. My academic and personal fascination with the power of the mind to heal led to an exploration of the role of imagination in healing. Images, of course, come from many sources: from our personal memories, from what Swiss psychiatrist C.G. Jung called the "collective unconscious" that is available to all, and from what we see and experience in the world around us. Negative images create fear which can also affect the body negatively. Hopeful images, in contrast, can bring forth the love and peace of mind that optimize physical health and support the process of healing. Studies indicate that hospitalized patients whose rooms have a view of nature (a healing image) mend faster and are released from the hospital sooner than patients who view brick walls. These kinds of studies have prompted many hospitals to incorporate healing images through architecture, plantings, music and art. I first heard of Joan Drescher in connection with a colorful border of kites that she had designed for the Joint Center for Radiation Therapy at Boston's Children's Hospital.

After I retired from academic medicine in 1988 to write, teach and follow my muse, Joan and I met at an ecumenical spiritual center on Boston's south shore where we both live. Within a few months we found ourselves in a women's meditation and prayer group together and an endless string of coincidences began to unfold. I would "lead" a meditation and it would turn out that the images that came to me were simultaneously in Joan's mind. She would share her healing art and poems would come alive in my mind. We would sit together silently and when one of us began to talk, the other would have been thinking the same thought.

It is a convenience of expression to say that I wrote the text and Joan illustrated the book. Both the text and the images were presented to us from a Higher Source that we both tapped into concurrently. As we worked on this book separately it was as if we were together. I had the good fortune to write the last portion of the text on a mini-retreat on the island of Kauai, on Hawaii. Several new ideas came to me which meant eliminating some of the previous images we had decided upon and substituting new ones. I called Joan, half a world away, hoping to get to her before she completed the previously agreed upon illustrations. She had in fact finished the illustrations, but they were the new ones that had come as strongly to her as to me!

The moment finally came for us to deliver this book to our publisher. I was to pick Joan up at 5:30 AM so we could board a 6:25 express train from Boston to New York—a challenge since neither of us are early risers. I set the alarm with care for 4:30, leaving fifteen extra minutes before I would really have to crawl out of bed at 4:45. Unfortunately, in the wee hours of the previous night I had erroneously set the alarm for 5:30! This was no problem for the Universe. At exactly 4:45 the phone rang and a soft, musical male voice spoke the single word, "Okay." And I was awake. A coincidence? An angel? A miracle? Such little gifts have made this book a delight to create. We offer it to you with the hope that you will experience the same power of love and awakening in working with it as we have in creating it.

About Participating in This Book

My creative mentor, guide and role model is an eleventh-century healer, the Abbess Hildegard Von Bingen. She was a physician and a scientist who described the circulation of the blood well before Sir William Harvey. She was also a mystic and visionary who saw through windows of time into eternity and directly perceived the luminous web of love in which we live and move and have our being. Hildegard believed that a complete cosmology consisted of science, healthy mysticism and art. For art, she maintained, is the true awakener of the people.

During Hildegard's visions she heard celestial music which she wrote down and to which I often listened as I worked on the text. You might enjoy listening to her music as well. Two cassettes are available, "A Feather on the Breath of God" and "Symphoniae: Spiritual Songs." I also enjoyed listening to "Rhythm of Life," the inspired ecumenical spiritual music of Gordon Burnham who is the Musical Director of the Vedanta Center where Joan and I first met. Joan Drescher was particularly inspired by Paul Winter's "Missa Gaia-Earth Mass," one of my meditation tapes, "The Harmony of Opposites," and "Drawing from the Light Within" by Judith Cornell as she worked on the illustrations. Perhaps you have favorite music that moves you beyond the limits of this world and opens your heart to an expanded reality. If so, you might enjoy listening to it while you work with the book. Ordering information for some of our favorite music, meditation tapes and information on Joan's healing murals which have been reproduced as wallpaper can be found on the last page of this book.

Joan and I have created images in pictures and words that are meant to awaken images that come from you and from the One Mind. The book consists of two basic parts. The first part asks the question, "Can you remember?" and invites you to retrieve memories and images from your personal past and from our collective unconscious as human beings. While we don't expect your conscious mind to actually remember what it felt like in your baby body, or by the ancestral fires when our species were hunter-gatherers, your "other-than-conscious" mind knows all this and more. You can tune into this larger mind by taking your time as you experience each invitation to remember, and noticing how your body, your breathing and your feelings respond. You may feel little tingles of recognition, flutterings of "aha" in your solar plexus, warmth in your heart. These are the seeds of awakening that any good story, work of art or sharing from the heart can plant. It is then up to you to nourish the growing seedlings of awareness.

The second part of the book consists of meditations and attitudes about life that will help you nourish the seeds of awakening. These invitations to remain awake are signaled by the shift in the text from "Can you remember?" to "I can remember." Take your time as you participate with these aids to remembering. As you become more familiar with the text you may want to close your eyes for some of the meditations. As they become your own you can do them anytime, anyplace. The fruits of these practices are sweet: self-acceptance, creativity, empowerment, joy, compassion, forgiveness, gratitude and peace of mind. These are your birthright and we hope that this book will encourage you to claim these gifts of Spirit.

The art in this book is itself a meditation. Beauty is a sure and subtle awakener that brings forth hope and wholeness. Allow yourself to be drawn in by the beauty; to become one with the images. You might then enjoy closing your eyes and relaxing into the inner imagery that the color, shapes and archetypal symbols in the art may have evoked. Symbols are a powerful shorthand that your other-than-conscious mind immediately recognizes: symbols can be profoundly strengthening and inspiring. Perhaps you will find special ones that you can carry with you in your mind or re-create by drawing or by clipping out similar symbols from books and magazines.

On some pages the art is less detailed and you will find simple color washes. Allow these abstract swirls of color to draw you inward, to comfort you, to reawaken your memories. Throughout the text there are also affirmations, indicated by italics, that can aid the process of remembering. The affirmations are like summary statements of the insights and awakenings that Joan and I experienced through the text and images we co-created. By repeating these affirmations out loud as you come to them, and by pausing to feel them in your body, you may experience the same feelings that Joan and I did. You may also come up with your own affirmations as your images mingle with ours to awaken memories that are unique to your own process of remembering. You may want to write down any such affirmations and use them as reminders for yourself whenever the stream of daily worries, concerns and fears puts you back to sleep again.

Affirmations can be as short as a word like breathe, or peace, or love or as long as a poem. They are actually prayers — statements of longing and intent — that invite grace into our lives and ignite the creative power of love in the service of awakening. This poem, which I first wrote and published in Guilt Is the Teacher, Love

<u>Is the Lesson</u>, initiated the chain of grace that led to the publication of this book. Your own poems, too, can invoke magic.

In the secret recesses of the heart
beyond the teachings of this world
calls a still, small voice
singing a song unchanged
from the foundation of the world.
Speak to me in sunsets and in starlight
Speak to me in the eyes of a child
You Who call from a smile
My cosmic beloved
Tell me who I am
And who I always will be.

—Joan Borysenko

In fact, any work of creativity invokes magic—both in the one who creates and in the one or many who receive.

The creation of art for this book has been filled with magic and miracles too numerous to describe. The alchemy of co-creation was catalyzed by love and the wish to be of service. Its beauty has taught me to trust in the Universe, follow my heart, and draw from the Light within. My hope is that the Divine Light that has touched me while painting will inspire and heal you.

—*Joan Drescher*

On Wings of Light

Once upon a time
love erupted with a mighty roar.
A ball of living, breathing light
exploded into a universe
of fire and ice, suns and moons, plants and animals,
you and me.
Since that first moment
love has known itself and expanded itself
through us.
Our joys and sorrows, hopes and fears,
our dissolution in night's soft womb
and re-creation in the morning's song
are reflections of the divine love
that plays its infinite melodies
on the tender strings of our hearts.
The notes of anguish, exultation and anger
delight, pain and grace unite in a
sacred harmony when we remember that
behind all appearances
beyond the illusion of separateness
We are One.

In that remembering
we can rejoice in our divine birthright
as children of love's first light.
Come
and let us remember together.

Take a deep breath and let your body relax . . .
feel yourself sinking into the arms of matter
all the while remembering your divine Source.

I am a bridge between heaven and earth.
The love of creation flows through me.

Can you remember arriving from the far corners of the universe
and tucking your lightself into human form?

Take a deep breath and let your body relax . . .
remember your baby body.
Feel its life and promise.
Feel its peace and power.

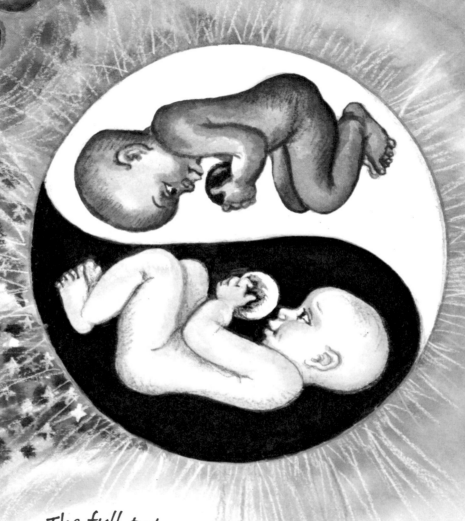

The full potential of the universe is present within me.

Can you remember what your favorite story was when you were in your child body?
Take your time and bring your awareness to each image.
Notice the way that your breath and body respond.

Take a deep breath and let your body relax . . .
feel the magic and mystery of the stories deep within.

I am a being of power, radiance and mystery.

Life is a creative adventure.

Can you remember when we sat by the fire and told
stories of the hunt, stories of the sky,
stories of the Great Mother who gives and nourishes life?

I am safe in the arms
of mother earth
and grandfather sky.

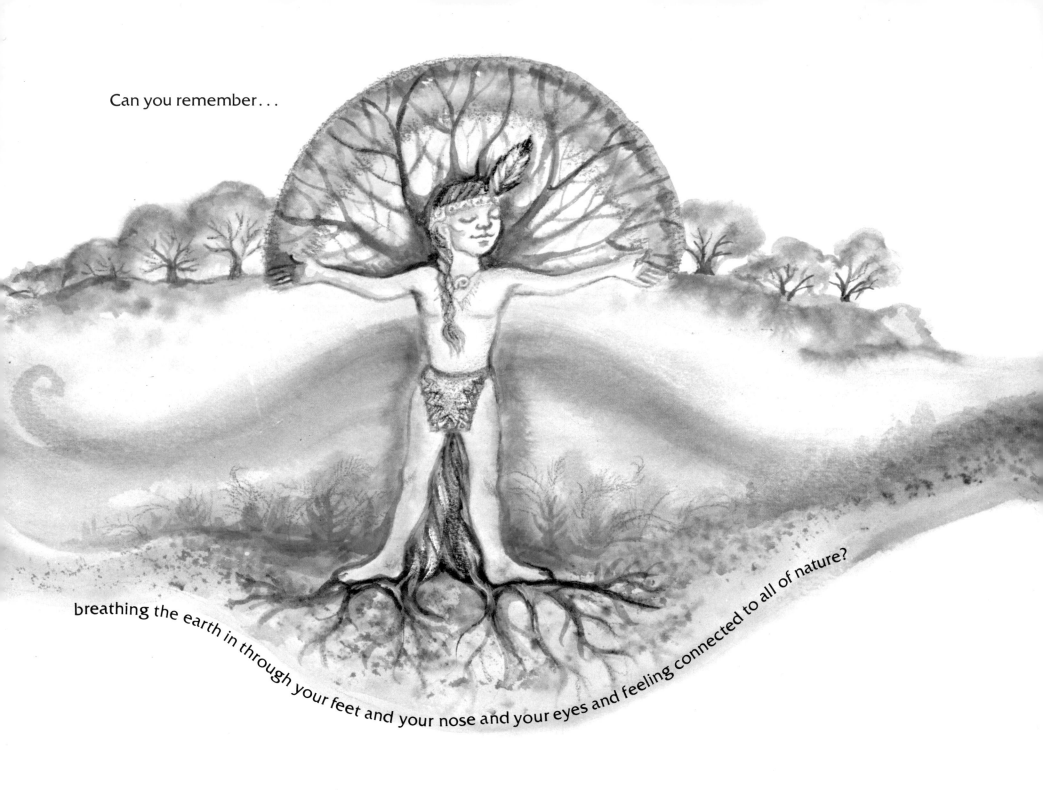

Can you remember . . .

breathing the earth in through your feet and your nose and your eyes and feeling connected to all of nature?

Take a deep breath and let your body relax . . .
remember a time when your whole body resonated
with the pulse of the earth.

I am connected to all that is, at one with the wholeness of life.

Can you remember
when you fell asleep
to the radiance and memories
that you are?
When you forgot the stories
of our ancestors
the lullabies of our mother
the magic of our childhood?

When did you come to believe
in the lies of darkness,
the illusion that you are isolated,
unworthy, unlovable
or otherwise separate
from the Whole?

It is time to wake up again
and to remember who I really am.

Feel life arising freshly within you, awakening your memories.
Take a deep breath and feel the lifeforce in your body.

I am a child of the one light,
a bridge between heaven and earth.
When love flows across that bridge
miracles happen.

I can travel the universe on wings of light
as long as I remember
my connection to the source of our being.

I can remember by paying attention to my breath.
Become aware of the flow of your breathing
        breathe light in through the top of your head
        breathe light out through the soles of your feet.

                Sense the inner tides as your whole body
                swells with the inbreath, lets go with the outbreath.

                        The ancient marriage of earth and sky, moon and sea
                        is consummated in the sacred rhythm of your breath.
                        Take time to be present to the flow.

Earth and sky, fire and water, spirit and matter
unite in me.
My breath is one with the heartbeat of the universe.

I can remember by reflecting on a time when I was completely present to life.

A holy moment. A time when the mystery revealed itself to me in
the eyes of a child, or the light of the moon resting on the
breast of the sea. A time when a glimpse of starlight, the
colors of a rainbow or the face of my beloved became the whole
of eternity.

Take a deep breath and let your body relax
think back to a time when you felt at one with nature, yourself, a pet or another person
go inside yourself, closing your eyes if your like.
Remember the sights . . . the sounds . . . the fragrances . . . the sensations.

The peace, love, gratitude and joy that these memories awaken
are your own true nature, your highest self. It is through that
self that we help bring the world into being. It is in that self
that we are most fully human and most completely divine.

The whole of eternity is present in each moment.
When I live my life one moment at a time
one breath at a time,
I live from my highest self which is one with all.

I can remember by paying attention to what is
rather than living in the movies of my mind.

Pretend that you are a stranger in a strange land.
Engage your full attention by focusing on your breathing . . .
now open your senses newly to the world around you.
Take several minutes to notice:

What do you see?
What do you hear?
What do you touch?
What do you feel?
What do you know in your heart?

Peace of mind is my own true nature
I claim it by letting go of the past and future
paying attention to what is.

I can remember by embracing every activity as sacred.

Sewing on a button, working in the garden, doing the wash, driving down the freeway, going to work.

To be present is to be joyful.
To be joyful is to radiate love.
To radiate love is to heal and be healed.

I am present to all things, all circumstances
and all people without judgment.
I can see God in everything.

I can remember by taking responsibility when I act out of ignorance or fear, and then forgiving myself.

I accept my errors as teachings in wisdom and compassion.

I can remember by expressing lovingkindness.

Take a deep breath and relax your body as you exhale slowly.
Imagine that you are standing in a beam of sunlight.

Think of all the things you have experienced in this lifetime.
Joy and sorrow, wonder and sadness, love and loss, births and deaths.

Bring to mind the child you once were and with reverence,
respect and love for all that child has endured in its search for wisdom.
Repeat these lovingkindness blessings for yourself.

May I be at peace.
May my heart remain open.
May I remember the beauty of my own true nature.
May I express my fullest potential.
May I be healed.

Imagine your loved ones, one by one, or in a group standing in the beam of sunlight.

May you be at peace.
May your heart remain open.
May you remember the beauty of your own true
nature.
May you be healed.

Imagine any person or persons that you are in conflict with standing in the beam of sunlight.

May you be at peace.
May your heart remain open.
May you remember the beauty of your own true
nature.
May you be healed.

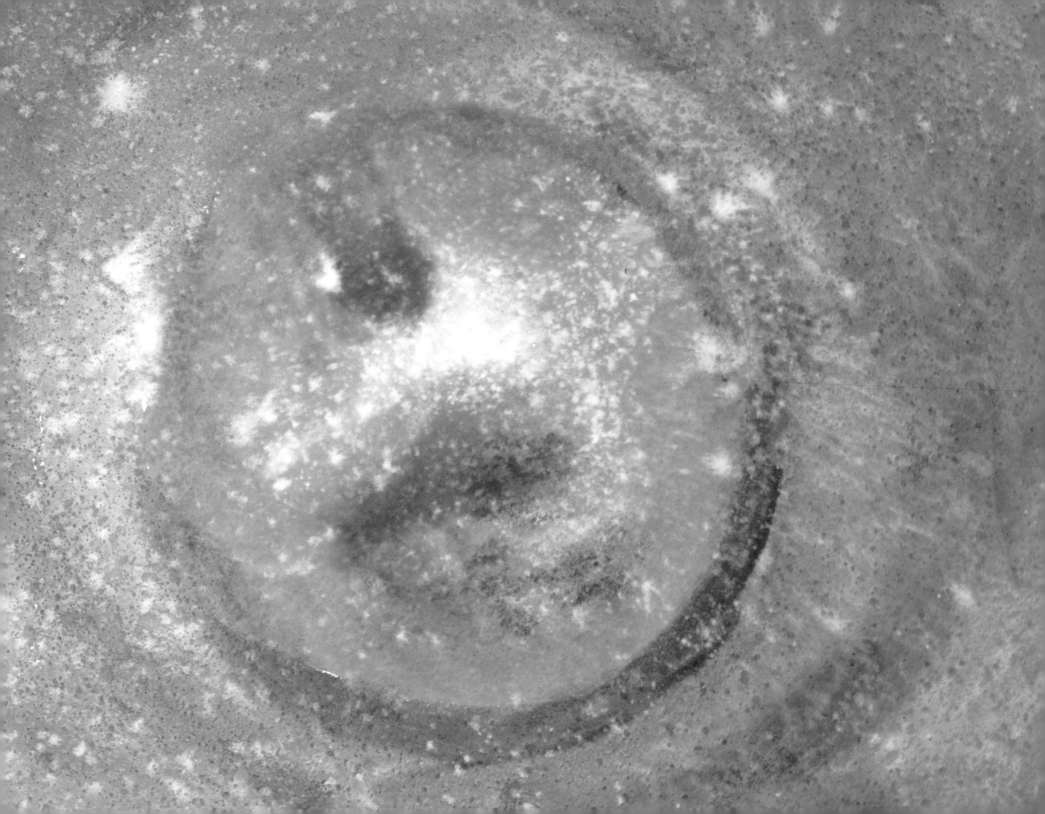

Imagine our beautiful earth,
hanging like a jewel in the starry vastness of space.

The blue seas, the green continents,
the white clouds.

A living, breathing being of
fire and water...earth and sky...
minerals and plants...
animals and human beings.

May there be peace on earth.   May the hearts of all people be open to one another.

May all life reach its highest potential.   May all life reflect the glory of the light.

I can remember by believing
that whatever is happening
no matter how strange, or sad, or painful
is happening in love's service.
I am perfectly and eternally safe.

The radiance that tucked itself into my baby body
and my child body.
The radiance of love, wisdom and creation
is still present within me.

It was present before my body was
and will be present when my body is no more.
It is present in the fire, in the stories,
in the ancestors and the stars.

It is present as who I am and
evermore shall be.
The Great One
who is ever reflecting life
back to itself as itself.

I am the soul of the world
and the Song of Songs.
My life is a wonder and a blessing.

I need only remember.

For information on ordering music tapes, Joan Borysenko's meditation tapes
or Joan Drescher's healing murals or wallpaper contact
Mind/Body Health Sciences, Inc. 22 Lawson Terrace, Scituate, MA 02066; (617) 545-7122.